Eddie's Little Sister Makes a Splash

By **Ed Koch** and **Pat Koch Thaler**

Illustrated by **James Warhola**.

G. P. Putnam's Sons

G. P. PUTNAM'S SONS
A division of Penguin Young Readers Group.
Published by The Penguin Group.
Penguin Group (USA) Inc., 375 Hudson Street, New York, NY 10014, U.S.A.
Penguin Group (Canada), 90 Eglinton Avenue East, Suite 700, Toronto, Ontario, Canada M4P 2Y3
(a division of Pearson Penguin Canada Inc.).
Penguin Books Ltd, 80 Strand, London WC2R 0RL, England.
Penguin Ireland, 25 St. Stephen's Green, Dublin 2, Ireland (a division of Penguin Books Ltd.).
Penguin Group (Australia), 250 Camberwell Road, Camberwell, Victoria 3124, Australia
(a division of Pearson Australia Group Pty Ltd).
Penguin Books India Pvt Ltd, 11 Community Centre, Panchsheel Park, New Delhi - 110 017, India.
Penguin Group (NZ), Cnr Airborne and Rosedale Roads, Albany, Auckland 1310, New Zealand
(a division of Pearson New Zealand Ltd).
Penguin Books (South Africa) (Pty) Ltd, 24 Sturdee Avenue, Rosebank, Johannesburg 2196, South Africa.
Penguin Books Ltd, Registered Offices: 80 Strand, London WC2R 0RL, England.

Library of Congress Cataloging-in-Publication Data
Koch, Ed, 1924–
Eddie's little sister makes a splash / by Ed Koch and Pat Koch Thaler ; illustrated by James Warhola.
p. cm.   Summary: Patty wants very much to act like a big girl when her family goes on vacation,
but at age five-and-a-half, she mostly manages to pester her older brother.
1. Koch, Ed, 1924– —Childhood and youth—Juvenile fiction.
[1. Koch, Ed, 1924– —Childhood and youth—Fiction. 2. Brothers and sisters—Fiction.
3. Camps—Fiction. 4. Swimming—Fiction.] I. Thaler, Pat Koch. II. Warhola, James, ill. III. Title.
PZ7.K7885Edd 2007   [Fic]—dc22   2006008254

ISBN 978-0-399-24310-3
1 3 5 7 9 10 8 6 4 2
First Impression

Patty was excited as Mom and Dad and Eddie began to pack the car for vacation. Patty wanted to help too, so she tried to drag a suitcase to the car.

"Patty," said Eddie, "it's nice of you to want to help, but this job is for big kids. Just stay out of the way until we're finished." Eddie swung the suitcase up to the top of the car.

"Are we taking everything we own with us?" Patty asked Dad.

"Everything but the kitchen sink," he joked. "But it's all stuff we'll need for two weeks at the cabin."

"Wait, wait, Dad. I forgot something," Patty shouted, and ran back to the house. A minute later, carrying a little suitcase with her doll's name on it, she climbed back into the car.

"We're going on vacation and we'll have lots of fun," Patty said to Noony. "You can look out the window on the way."

"We're here," Eddie said when they got to Cabin 6. "Patty, we were in Cabin 3 last year. This one looks even better."

Patty didn't remember ever being here. Nothing looked familiar. The cabin looked scary. The beds had bare mattresses and there were no pictures on the wall.

Patty hugged Noony and whispered to her, "Don't be afraid. I'll take care of you."

"Eddie, please show Patty around while we unpack," Mom said. "See if you can find her some playmates. And be sure to bring her back soon, before it gets dark."

Patty and Eddie raced out the door. "I hope Noah and Benji are here," Eddie said.

A wide path led into the woods. "Where does that big path go?" Patty asked.

"That goes to the lake where we'll go swimming. But you must never, ever go by yourself. The water is very deep and you don't know how to swim," Eddie said.

At the ball field they met Noah and Benji.

"Hi, Eddie. Let's have a catch," said Noah.

"I don't have time tonight, fellas, but let's do something tomorrow,"
Eddie said. Then he remembered to ask his friends, "Are there any kids
here Patty's age? She's looking for a friend."

Benji and Noah shook their heads. "There are lots of families with babies. But I haven't seen any kids your size, Patty," said Benji.

"How old are you, anyway?" asked Noah.

Patty stood up very straight and said, "I'm five and one quarter. I have lots of friends in the city." And she began to count them. "There's Kayla, Jordan, Sasha, Hannah, Perri—"

"See you tomorrow, fellas," Eddie interrupted. "Come on, Patty," he said as he grabbed her hand.

"If I weren't dragging you along, I could have stayed with my friends. Starting tomorrow, I'll be out all day on my own and I don't want you following me around. Okay?"

"I don't want to play with you guys, anyway," Patty said, and ran toward the cabin.

Cabin 6 looked much cozier when they returned.
Patty's special blanket was on a bed in the room
she and Eddie would share.

When it was time for bed, Mom read
Patty a story and tucked her in,
just the way she did at home.

Patty could hear Eddie
talking to the grown-ups in the
other room. "I'll try and find
Patty a friend tomorrow," she
heard him say.

"Why does Eddie get to
stay up later than I do?" she
whispered to Noony. "I don't
need him to find me a
friend, anyway." Soon
she fell asleep in her
cabin bed.

The next morning, the bright sun woke Patty up. Eddie was just leaving to go swimming with his friends. Patty put on her swimsuit, grabbed her swim cap and a towel, tucked Noony under her arm, and ran to follow Eddie.

"Hey, sweetheart, what are you doing?" Dad asked.

"I'm going with Eddie," Patty said.

"But Patty, Eddie's much older than you. You can't go without Mom and me. Play on the swings and we'll take you to the lake soon."

Patty sat on one of the swings and Mom came over to give her a push. "You don't need to push me. I'm a big girl. I can do it myself."

"Yes. You certainly are a big girl. Stay near the cabin and play here by yourself for a little while. Then Dad and I will go to the lake with you."

From high on
the swing Patty could
see the path to the lake.
When she heard
children's voices,
she hopped off.

Maybe I'll find a friend to play
with, she thought. She remembered
what Mom had said about staying
near the cabin, but the voices didn't
sound too far away.

"I can find my own friends.
It won't take me long and then
I'll be back."

At the end of the path, Patty saw Eddie and his friends
having fun out in the lake.

Patty waved to Eddie, but he was too busy to notice her.
She took off her sandals and put on her swim cap.

"I'll just go as far as the end of this dock," she said. "Then Eddie will come and get me."

Patty waded into the water, holding on to the dock. The water was shallow near the shore.

But suddenly her feet were no longer touching the bottom. Her hand fell from the dock and a moment later her head was underwater. She bobbed up and managed to yell, "Eddie!" before she slipped under the water again.

She came to the surface once more and yelled, "Help!"

From the float, Eddie spotted Patty's swim cap and her head bobbing up and down in the water. "I'm coming, Patty," he yelled, and he swam as fast as he could.

Eddie grabbed Patty and pulled her out of the water.

"Patty, Patty—are you all right?" Eddie said.

Benji and Noah reached them just as Patty opened her eyes. She spit out a mouthful of water and began to cry.

Eddie wanted to be mad at Patty for not listening to the rules, but she looked so scared that he couldn't be angry.

As Patty brushed away her tears, Mom and Dad arrived. They were so glad that Eddie had saved Patty that they hugged and kissed them both. "I didn't know the water was so deep. I would have drowned if Eddie hadn't saved me," Patty told them. "But when I learn to swim, I'm going out to the float to jump off just like those big kids."

"I think it's time for you to take swimming lessons," Mom said.

"Yes," said Patty. "When I learn to swim, I'll be a really big girl!"

On the way back to the cabin, Patty remembered Noony. "Oh, she's all alone," she said, and ran to the swings, where she found Noony.

"You're a good girl," Patty said to Noony. "You listened and didn't go to the lake."

Early the next morning, Dad took Patty to the lake for her first swimming lesson.

Patty paddled around in the shallow water and blew bubbles underwater. After a few lessons she could really swim.

"You're a natural," Eddie said. "Next year, I'll take you out to the deep water." Patty felt very grown-up.

The day before vacation was over, Patty saw another girl in the shallow water and swam up to her.

"Hi, my name is Patty and I'm five and a quarter. How old are you?"

"I'm six and my name is Sally."

"I'm going home tomorrow," Patty said. "But we can play after my swim lesson." And they did.

When it was time to go, Patty got Noony ready. As they drove away, Patty said, "This was the best vacation of my whole life! I found a friend and I learned to swim."

Eddie smiled and said, "Just don't forget what happened at the lake."

"Oh, Eddie—I'll never forget you saved me," said Patty.

"I'll never forget either!" said Mom.

Dad laughed and said, "You certainly made a big splash!"

"And next summer, after a few more lessons, we can swim to the float together," said Eddie.